THE
GINGERBREAD MAN

For Deborah and Kimo

E. A. K.

For Kim, Leo, Chanté, and Bator—thanks for my
little gingerbread man, Yonder

M. L.

Text copyright © 1993 by Eric A. Kimmel
Illustrations copyright © 1993 by Megan Lloyd
All rights reserved
Printed and bound in June 2010 at Kwong Fat Offset Printing Co., Ltd.,
Dongguan City, Guang Dong Province, China.
Library of Congress Cataloging-in-Publication Data
Kimmel, Eric A.
The gingerbread man / written by Eric A. Kimmel:illustrated by Megan Lloyd—1st ed.
p.   cm.
Summary: A freshly baked gingerbread man escapes when he is taken
out of the oven and eludes a number of animals until he meets a clever fox.
ISBN 0-8234-0824-8
[1. Fairy tales.   2. Folklore.]   I. Lloyd, Megan, ill.   II. Title.
PZ8.K527G1   1993   90-33202   CIP   AC
398.21— dc20
ISBN 0-8234-1137-0 (pbk.)
12 14 16 15 13

ISBN-13: 978-0-8234-0824-5 (hardcover)
ISBN-13: 978-0-8234-1137-5 (pbk.)

THE GINGERBREAD MAN

retold by Eric A. Kimmel

illustrated by Megan Lloyd

Holiday House/New York

Once upon a time an old woman and an old man decided to make some gingerbread. First they mixed up the dough. Then they rolled it out on the table. Then they cut the dough into the shape of a gingerbread man. The old woman and the old man put the gingerbread man in the oven to bake.

He baked for a good long time. When he was done, the old woman and the old man let him cool a little. Then they decorated him with two licorice eyes, a mouth made of icing, and three peppermint buttons down the front of his shirt. As soon as they put on the last peppermint button, up jumped the gingerbread man. To their surprise he leaped off the table and ran out the door.

"Come back, Gingerbread Man, come back!" the old woman and the old man called as they ran after him.

But the gingerbread man ran faster.

"I'll run and run as fast as I can.
You can't catch me. I'm the gingerbread man!"

Down the road ran the gingerbread man. He ran past the pigsty where the old sow lay. "Slow down, Gingerbread Man. I want to talk to you," the old sow oinked. And she started running after the gingerbread man.

But the gingerbread man ran faster.

"I'll run and run as fast as I can.
You can't catch me. I'm the gingerbread man!
I ran from the woman. I ran from the man.
I'll run from you. See if I can!"

Down the road ran the gingerbread man. He ran past the doghouse. The dog wagged his tail. "Slow down, Gingerbread Man. I want to talk to you," the dog barked. And he started running after the gingerbread man.

But the gingerbread man ran faster.

"I'll run and run as fast as I can.
You can't catch me. I'm the gingerbread man!
I ran from the woman. I ran from the man.
I'll run from you. See if I can!"

Down the road ran the gingerbread man. He ran past the pasture where the horse and the cow stood grazing. The horse neighed. The cow mooed. "Slow down, Gingerbread Man. We want to talk to you." And they started running after the gingerbread man.

But the gingerbread man ran faster.

"I'll run and run as fast as I can.
You can't catch me. I'm the gingerbread man!
I ran from the woman. I ran from the man.
I'll run from you. See if I can!"

Down the road ran the gingerbread man with the horse and the cow, the dog and the sow, the old woman and the old man running behind him.

The gingerbread man ran and ran until he came to the river. There he stopped, wondering what to do.

"Hello, Gingerbread Man," a voice said.

It was a fox. The gingerbread man cried:

I'll run and run as fast as I can.
You can't catch me. I'm the gingerbread man!
I ran from the horse. I ran from the cow.
I ran from the dog. I ran from the sow.
I ran from the woman. I ran from the man.
I'll run from you. See if I can!"

The fox chuckled. "Why, Gingerbread Man, you don't have to run from me. I am your friend. I want to help you."

"How can you help me?" the gingerbread man asked the fox.

"Hop on my tail," the sly fox said. "I will carry you across the river. You will be safe on the other side."

The gingerbread man hopped on the fox's tail. The fox jumped in the river and started swimming across.

"Gingerbread Man, the water is rising. Hop on my back so your feet don't get wet," the fox called out.

The gingerbread man hopped on the fox's back. The fox swam on.

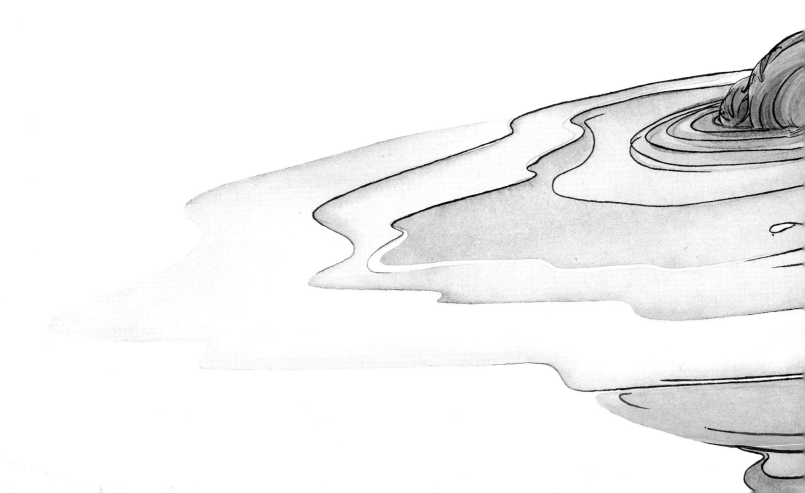

After a while the fox said, "Gingerbread Man, the water is still rising. Hop on my head so your feet don't get wet." The gingerbread man hopped on the fox's head. The fox swam on.

After a while the fox said again, "Gingerbread Man, the water is still rising. Hop on my snout so your feet don't get wet."
The gingerbread man hopped on the fox's snout.

But no sooner had he done that than. . .

the fox threw back his head and
snapped up the gingerbread man in one bite.

But don't be sad, for that wasn't the end of the gingerbread man.

The gingerbread man has gone away,
But he'll be back some other day.
For gingerbread men return, it's said,
When someone bakes some gingerbread.